# APPLEBAUMS HAVE A ROBOT!

## JANE THAYER ⊘ illustrated by Bari Weissman

William Morrow and Company    New York  1980

Printed in the United States of America.
1 2 3 4 5 6 7 8 9 10


Library of Congress Cataloging in Publication Data

Woolley, Catherine.
   Applebaums have a robot!
Summary: A young robot finds his vocation in a bakery
and earns a baker's hat as the result of his devoted work.
[1. Robots—Fiction. 2. Bakers and bakeries—Fiction]
I. Weissman, Bari. II. Title.
PZ7.W882Ap  [E]  79-28065
ISBN 0-688-22231-5   ISBN 0-688-32231-X (lib. bdg.)

In a family of robots the youngest was called So-On.
His real name was X-Y-8-9-10-Z,
but everyone said, "X-Y-and-So-On."

So-On was born in a factory,
and his parents were the Robot Makers.
The Makers made sure their robot children
had all their buttons and wires.
They even gave So-On—since he was the youngest—
an extra wire or two.
One by one the robots were ready
to begin their work in the world.
"What career appeals to you?" Mr. Maker asked the oldest.

"Work in a factory. Invent new methods,"
the oldest beeped back.
"I'm proud of you!" said his father.
The next one said, "I'm going to work on solar energy."
"A career in science. How wonderful!" said her mother.
So it went. "I would like to work on water power."
"I'm going to the Milky Way."
"Did you ever see such a brilliant family!"
the Makers marveled.

Then they said, "So-On, what about you, dear?"

So-On was small for a robot,

and he didn't feel brilliant at all.

"Perhaps you'd like to join your brother in industry?"

"No."

"Or go into solar science?"

"No!"

"Don't you want to go to the Milky Way?"

"Oh, no!" cried So-On.

"I just want a job in some nice place!"

His parents looked at each other.

"Let's face it," said Mr. Maker.

"We have one child with no ambition."

"Don't you want a distinguished career?" Ms. Maker cried.

So-On clanged his foot down.

"Are you sure he has all his buttons?" asked his father.

"Something's gone wrong," agreed his mother.

"Well, we want you to be happy, dear."

"But useful," said his father. "Robots must be useful."

So-On wanted to be useful, but he wanted to be happy, too.

He drifted along.

He did housework, but the dust made him squeak.

He delivered mail in a factory, but factory work bored him.

He guarded a bank and he liked chasing robbers,
but not many robbers came.
One day, however, So-On did chase a robber,
and the chase led past Applebaums' Bakery.
Something smelled delicious.

So-On forgot about the robber and stopped.
He stepped inside and was greeted by
the fragrance of fresh bread and pies and cinnamon buns.
The bakery was cheerful with sunshine,
warm from the ovens.

He rushed home.
"I wish I could work in Applebaums' Bakery!"
The Makers were shocked. Their robot in a bakery?
When all the other children were launched on great careers?
But they were good parents, so they said, "Apply for a job."

The baker was a little man,
round and plump as his rising dough.
"What could a robot do in my bakery?" he inquired.
"Put bread in oven, watch, take out," So-On said eagerly.
"My wife and I have been thinking of hiring a helper,"
Mr. Applebaum said.
"But I can't afford a robot!"
"Work hard!" cried So-On.
"Well....What's your name?"
"X-Y-8-9-10-Z."
"That's a name? That's a number," the baker said.
"I'll call you Doughy. Okay, we'll try it."
Doughy rushed to tell the Makers.
"Come here and be programmed," they said.
They arranged two buttons
so he could put the bread in the oven
and take it out golden brown.
Doughy was happy and excited.
In fact, he was so happy that just as he left
he said he must have one more button.
Ms. Maker gave it to him.

Mr. Applebaum pressed two buttons,
and Doughy started his job.
"Fine," said the baker.
"What's this other button?" He pressed it.

Doughy began to sing.
"So happy!" he told them. "Burst if I don't sing!"
The Applebaums were delighted.
Doughy loved his job.

In the warm, sunny bakery with its good smells,
he put the bread and buns in the oven
and took them out golden brown.
"Applebaums have a robot?" said the customers.
They came to watch him work.

Mr. Applebaum had to make
many more loaves of bread and buns,
and Mrs. Applebaum made apple pies all day.
"Whew!" said the baker.
"I wish Doughy could mix the bread for us."

Doughy was eager to please because he loved the bakery.

He rushed back to the Makers on his day off.

"Two more arms! Left side," he ordered.

"Two arms, left side." They operated.

He showed Mr. Applebaum.

"Four hands! Make bread, tend ovens."

"Imagine!" marveled the Applebaums,

and Mr. Applebaum stopped mixing bread dough.

Doughy was so happy that he tossed the dough in the air.
Mr. Applebaum made hundreds of cinnamon buns
to meet the demand.
"If only Doughy could make the buns too," he said with a sigh.
Doughy loved his job and the bakery and the Applebaums,
and he wanted to please.
He rushed to the Makers. "Two more arms! Right side."
Onto the operating table.

Now Doughy did everything but make the pies.
And so many people came to see the six-armed singing robot
and to buy bread and buns and pies
that even with Doughy's help the bakery couldn't keep up.
In fact, nice Mr. Applebaum was so overworked
that he became ill-tempered.

"Can't you work faster?" he snapped at Doughy.
"Come on, Doughy! Step on it, Doughy!
These people are waiting, Doughy!"
Doughy was trying so hard to keep up
that his left hands didn't know
what his right hands were doing.

His robot brain grew confused.
His robot brain began to break down.
And finally he let an ovenful of bread burn up.
Mr. Applebaum shouted, and Doughy collapsed.

His last thought as he fainted away was
Mr. Applebaum will sell me for junk.
A robot technician came. "Needs rest," he said.
Rest didn't help.

They shot high-voltage current through Doughy.
Didn't help.

They took Doughy away.

The Applebaums had all the work to do once more,
and they had many more customers now.
They became very tired.
Finally they got a new robot, named Q-P-T-G-J.
He was a later model.

"He can't sing," said Mrs. Applebaum.
"See how many loaves he can handle!"
her husband pointed out.
"I miss Doughy," said Mrs. Applebaum. "I loved Doughy."
"Business is booming!" her husband pointed out.

Business did boom, until one day a customer said,
"The bread doesn't taste the same."
Mr. Applebaum protested. "Same recipe, same ovens."
Business began to fall off.
The baker tasted the bread.
"They're right. Something is missing," he said.
"What can be missing?"
"Love," said Mrs. Applebaum.

"Doughy put love in his loaves."
Her husband stared at her.
"You are right! And I miss Doughy too.
Maybe we can find another robot
who will love this place as he did."
They asked the Makers,
"Have you got another singing robot like Doughy?"
"No," said the Makers.

"But we've got Doughy!
He is practically well,
but he can never work so hard again."
"That's all right!" Mr. Applebaum shouted.
"We want him back!"
"We'll all slow down," his wife promised.
"We don't need so much business."
They found a job for Q-P-T-G-J on a distant star
and took Doughy back to the bakery.
He felt better at once.
"Get more hands! Make pies too!"
he told Mr. Applebaum eagerly.
"Now, Doughy," said his boss,
"you don't need hands coming out of your head.
What would Mrs. Applebaum and I do if you did all the work?"
"We love to roll out rich piecrust,
slice juicy apples," Mrs. Applebaum told him.
"And here is something to celebrate your coming home,"
Mr. Applebaum said.
He set a high, white, handsome hat on Doughy's head.

Doughy, in his high white hat, stood speechless with joy.
Then, without a new button,
without being programmed, he made a miracle.
He burst into a new song.
Mr. and Mrs. Applebaum sang, too.

Pictures of Doughy, the six-armed robot,
who was back at Applebaums
in his high, white, handsome hat,
appeared in the papers.
Mr. and Mrs. Maker cut out the pictures.

"We have wonderful robot children!"
they told their friends.
"One makes a gas-free car.
One is in solar science.
One has a beautiful home in the Milky Way.
And our little So-On!"
they said tenderly, showing a picture of Doughy.
"He is now a partner in that world-famous little bakery. . .

149094